Mr. Gumpy's Outing

John Burningham

HOLT, RINEHART AND WINSTON

New York   Chicago   San Francisco

Other books by John Burningham

BORKA

TRUBLOFF

ABC

HUMBERT

CANNONBALL SIMP

HARQUIN

SEASONS

Friezes by John Burningham

BIRDLAND

LIONLAND

STORYLAND

JUNGLELAND

WONDERLAND

Originally published in England by Jonathan Cape Ltd.
Copyright © 1970 by John Burningham
All rights reserved, including the right to reproduce
this book or portions thereof in any form.
Published simultaneously in Canada by Holt, Rinehart
and Winston of Canada, Limited.
ISBN: 0-03-086612-X (Trade)
ISBN: 0-03-086613-8 (HLE)
Library of Congress Catalog Card Number: 77-159507
Printed in the United States of America
First American Edition
Typography and title-page design by Jan Pienkowski

This is Mr. Gumpy.

Mr.Gumpy owned a boat and his house
was by a river.

One day Mr. Gumpy went out in his boat.

"May we come with you?" said the children.

"Yes," said Mr. Gumpy,
"if you don't squabble."

"Can I come along, Mr. Gumpy?"
said the rabbit.

"Yes, but don't hop about."

"I'd like a ride," said the cat.

"Very well," said Mr.Gumpy.
"But you're not to chase the rabbit."

"Will you take me with you?" said the dog.

"Yes," said Mr. Gumpy.
"But don't tease the cat."

"May I come, please, Mr. Gumpy?"
said the pig.

"Very well, but don't muck about."

"Have you a place for me?" said the sheep.

"Yes, but don't keep bleating."

"Can we come too?" said the chickens.

"Yes, but don't flap," said Mr. Gumpy.

"Can you make room for me?" said the calf.

"Yes, if you don't trample about."

"May I join you, Mr. Gumpy?" said the goat.

"Very well, but don't kick."

For a little while they all went along happily but then...

The goat kicked

The calf trampled

The chickens flapped

The sheep bleated

The pig mucked about

The dog teased the cat

The cat chased the rabbit

The rabbit hopped

The children squabbled

The boat tipped...

and into the water they fell.

Then Mr. Gumpy and the goat and the calf and the chickens and the sheep and the pig and the dog and the cat and the rabbit and the children all swam to the bank and climbed out to dry in the hot sun.

"We'll walk home across the fields," said Mr. Gumpy. "It's time for tea."

"Goodbye," said Mr. Gumpy.
"Come for a ride another day."